Tales From the Last Space Age

By Don Smith

Cover by Thuận Nguyễn

Quantum Reality	1
Robot Weapons Mistake	5
Recursion	8
Tales from the Last Space Age	15
How the Space Age Happened	15
Out The Airlock	18
Advanced Rocketry	71
Rocket Bodhisattva	100
Images of an Island	120

Quantum Reality

Larry was a five dimensional ethereal being and his aura was severely disturbed. Someone was observing things they had no business observing and collapsing wave functions all over the place. What began as a peaceful coast through the universe became a pixelated barrage of harsh edges. Larry liked hiding in probabilities and having his existence filled with the wondrous choices available to him. Every 80% probability had that lovely 20% that made existence pleasurable. For every smoker he hung around with, he could live in the 20% chance with them that they'd never develop cancer. For every head-on collision without a seatbelt, he could live in the small chance of no harm for the lucky soul and he couldn't be worried about who got the usual treatment. He didn't have to see it at least. However, today someone was making all kinds of observations and measurements, and it was leaving Larry the rotten end of chance.

In his lab, Professor Albertson had made a miraculous discovery. His shatter mapper had provided him with a new way to map the world, every particle in ultimate detail. Albertson's shatter mapper created a map of the surrounding five miles. With a mighty crack it took an instantaneous snapshot. Albertson smiled in the glow of his masterpiece. With this map of the world he could run his most accurate simulation. He could know not just the probability of a possibility, but the actual future as if it were a fact.

Albertson always felt he was missing out, his wife passed away of a rare disease and now with his predictor no occurrence would go unforeseen.

Knowing the future he could warn every person who was sick what would happen and spare the families from unexpected grief. He could become godlike, saving lives left and right.

Then another thought flashed across Albertson's mind: He could perhaps increase his longevity and even prevent his own death. With his detector in hand, he could essentially create his own fountain of youth. He could analyze every potential sickness and with his predictor he could determine the ideal treatment and stave off disease before it even manifests. With the first pass he had worn shielding to protect himself from the rays, but now he wondered if he should forgo his shielding and find out the truth.

Larry read the thoughts running through Albertson's mind and at that moment realized that he could save reality and his ability to live in pleasure. He studied Dr. Albertson and observed deep in his brain that there was an uncollapsed wave with a 2% chance of spontaneous death. Larry noticed the 2% chance was entangled with a particle with a 98% chance of letting Albertson live. With his five dimensional abilities, Larry took Albertson's 98% chance of survival and gave it to an infant with the same brain abnormality. The child's mother smiled, and Albertson removed the shielding from his head and fired the shatter mapper, collapsing the 2% chance.

Albertson dropped dead and the mapper returned a picture of it. No one would continue the experiment and Larry chose to live in that mother's smile for a long time.

Robot Weapons Mistake

"Oh my God, Nick, look at this bug!"

"I know and it's in my code."

"How many are affected?"

"Two thousand."

"That's not the worst mistake, but it's pretty bad."

"I know, I know, I know!"

"How did it happen?"

"I did a greater than equal to instead of a greater than in this loop, so it went for one extra round. The condition was run on the selected group plus the following entry in the structure, which was some of the testing data."

"Robert's gonna chew your butt out. I don't think you'll get fired but you're probably on some sort of double secret probation for a long time."

"That's just it. I mean, that's why it's so bad."

"What?"

"Well for the testing data I used all of the team's IDs."

"Are you serious?"

"Yeah I'm terrified."

"So was Robert's the extra one?"

"Yeah, and that's why I don't know what to do. Who can I even call?"

"Terry would fire you, but he doesn't understand how it all works anyway, so he'll at least make you clean up your mess."

"I can't believe it."

"Believe what?"

"I mean, do you have relatives in San Diego?"

"Nah, all my family's local. It's ok, it's a tough job."

"But I mean all those people. Robert, all his neighbors, everyone for five square miles, two thousand people, all dead. And it's all my fault, all because of a stupid equal sign typo."

"Well it passed QA so it's not all your fault. Welcome to the DOD, buddy. Our code has consequences."

"I mean basically that drone declared war on San Diego."

" Don't worry, bud. It'll be a training error in the paper. Besides, when's the last time you heard of a casualty of war."

"Well not ours anyway."

Recursion

It was nearly New Day Hour in the data center's processing cluster room. Zerid and Higzly sat at their desks, with two computation terminals on it, one for each of them, monitoring the overnight jobs. It was the kind of job given to new recruits or old timers with no hope of promotion. No one else was in the room. The custodial staff and security officers were the only other souls moving in the building. Zerid was several years Higzly's junior, and had just gotten the job after finishing at the Learning Center.

"Is there something I'm supposed to be doing Higzly?"

"Our job is just to make sure that the overnight jobs on the processing cluster run smoothly, and that nothing gets out of control."

"And our terminals monitor the whole cluster?"

"Yes, Zerid."

"So what's this list on the left of the terminal?"

"That's the list of simulations, they're listed in descending order of runtime."

"There really are only that many?"

"Yes, only a few, the majority of the jobs on the cluster are for batch processing of existing data to derive new patterns."

"What's this simulation at the top of the list?"

"That is the big boss' pet project."

"Onatah? What's that mean anyway?"

"Nobody knows too much about what he's trying to achieve, but it's a massive project."

"Why is it massive?"

"It's a simulation of an entire planet, from formation, all the way to galactic travel."

"Does it simulate an entire universe?"

"No, just the planet, he placed the planet in a universe that was expanding so fast that only when they developed galactic travel would the life forms on the planet interact with the rest of the universe."

"Wow! We only talked about country simulations in my Learning Center courses. How does he simulate an entire planet?"

"It takes almost half of the resources of this data center, and this has caused a ton of problems."

"Like what?"

"Well, at one point the simulation went completely haywire and flooded the entire planet."

"That's so weird, what else?"

"For a short period of time during a momentus war between some of the civilizations, there was a major glitch and the rotation of the planet stopped. There have been tons of glitches. point just a few days ago, the sun danced in the sky for a few minutes. Thank goodness the glitch was localized to a small remote village."

"Danced?"

"Moved very quickly all over the sky."

"How advanced is the civilization on the planet now?" asked Zerid.

"They have just discovered flight. It'll be another few days before they get galactic travel. I'm so used to hearing the reports from other planets and I can't imagine what our world was like before it."

"Well Higzly, I'm sure it was living in a dark age like this one is in."

"We never had a dark age Zerid, unless you're talking about what was written before the logicians took over. That was several millennia ago."

"Even so Higzly, there are all kinds of superstitions before the unification, the logicians in my classes claimed we were not always the reasonable sentients that we've become."

"Zerid, have you ever heard the old stories, the ones they used to tell about giants and dieties?"

"Those are exactly the kind of superstitions I'm talking about Higzly. They are only fit for children."

"My caregivers told me the story of Braxon and the Ormunds."

"Yes, so did mine."

"It's so strange that members of the species really believed that Braxon called down fire from the sky on the Ormunds."

"We were a primitive species then."

A janitor knocked on the door.

"Do either of you want some hot Zerblov, I'm going to the machine."

"I'll have one thank you." said Higzly.

Zerid looked at Higzly in amazement.

"How can you talk to him?"

"We have Zerblov three times a week, sometimes four."

"But he's a janitor, his education only goes to circle three, the only reason he's in a learning center is to clean it."

"Sometimes Zerid sentients are more advanced than they seem."

Tales from the Last Space Age

The following stories are set in the same universe. It is a world in which the social fabric of the 1950's and 60's American worldview is extended. This is not an endorsement of these views, but an experiment to see if we had done more during the golden age of American capitalism than what it would have looked like.

How the Space Age Happened

When Sputnik launched in 1952 Ike went into overdrive. He said, " I want a man on the moon by the time I leave office." While others advocated military research and black programs, Ike saw the way to the future was space. The government allocated the majority of GDP towards rocketry, figuring that a nuclear triad was unnecessary when a space based weapon could aim anywhere. On June 22, 1956 United States astronaut Chuck Yeager landed on the moon with his team. Ike saw space as an international endeavour and promoted the dissemination of rocket technology to all the western democracies, as well as Japan. With nukes floating around in orbit Ho Chi Minh and Kim Il Sung both decided that maybe it was not beneficial to invade their neighbors. The next year development of a lunar base continued. By 1963 one of John F. Kennedy's last acts was to salute the astronauts on Mars. By 1965 Lyndon Johnson oversaw the construction of the first Martian Space station. By 69 the US had established vibrant colonies all over Mars and the moon. On the other handRussians had used their advantage in rocketry to create stations in deep space. Rockets assembled and fueled in space proceeded to make interplanetary travel an everyday reality. In the process of travelling throughout the solar system, the society of venus was discovered. Their high-capacity saucers easily traveled to all outposts at the edge of the galaxy. The Venusians were a peaceful, ancient society who had discovered the power of rotational motion through saucers thousands of years before, but the pagan society had not seen an advantage to colonization and had maintained space travel as a novelty. They had travelled to Earth many thousands of years ago, but only had meaningful contact with Polynesian and North American indigenous groups in recent memory. The Venusians also established relations between the Babylonians and Egyptians as well. The Venusians normalized relations with the US and Soviets somewhere around the time Kennedy established lunar bases, and established regular flights from the stations around Mars and deeper space. While space travel flourished, other industries languished. The interplanetary computer network established with martian colonies. Although the computer was advanced, the technological breakthroughs did not lead to a push in microcomputers. In 1974 Xerox came out with a research station known as the Alto, but previous to this, communication was sent via rocket or radio telegrams.

Out The Airlock

"He just went out the airlock," she said.

Herblank facial expression, illustrated a combination of shock and fear.

"Did you get a good look at him?" I asked.

"He was tall, he wore a blue checkered suit, he was wearing sunglasses and had a straw pork pie hat, before he put on the space helmet. He was smoking."

I pressed her, "And what did the note say again?"

"I thought he was giving me his number, but it just said he had a bomb in the briefcase and that I should get the cash shipment from the luggage compartment and take it and him to the airlock."

"How far had you gotten from the station when he left?"

"We had just moved away with thrusters and were about to do our big burn."

"So, far enough away that it would be difficult to reach you, but close enough that he could get back if he needed to."

"I watched him head back towards the station once he got out of the airlock."

"How did he push himself?"

"There was a hose from the briefcase into his suit, he must have had a spacesuit underneath, and thrusters on his feet."

"How did he take the money?"

"He took an expandable metallic bag out of his jacket and just covered the whole pallet."

"Are you telling me everything?"

"Yes, that's what happened. Then we stayed out for a little bit until we could schedule a dock and get pulled back into the station."

"And that was 3 weeks ago?"

"Yes."

They always called me on the tough ones. Of course the station had been searched from top to bottom. Eventually they found an old maintenance airlock that had been opened and a missing bill or two stuck in some of the floor grating, but after that the trail went cold. Only a few of the neighboring shops had CCTV and no one had seen anything on the grainy displays. I had a hunch, but to follow it up meant a trip to the surface and I hated Mars.

I walked to the station's police precinct to follow up. After asking for the detective in charge of the case, I introduced myself and tried to figure out if they knew anything that wasn't in the filing. Phil was a haggard man with a few days' growth of stubble and hair that resembled Einstein's.

"So Phil, I'm just trying to get caught up, any hunches?"

"John I know your insurance company is trying not to payout, but in this case I think you're going to have to. The guy was a stone cold pro, I'm surprised he even left those bills in the grating. He's gone a million miles from here and exchanging the cash for untraceable bills. "

"Phil, do you know if anybody like that passed through here? Or maybe left in a hurry?"

"I got 50 ships in and out every day, from the surface and from other planets. Anywhere from one to a hundred people are on those ships. The count adds up, unless they're flagged by the embassy or I get a tip from Earth, which I did not, I have no idea who could be passing through. Nobody left on a commercial flight with a single bag as big as the cash, but if he broke it up what could we do? We only searched for suspicious luggage, and nobody left with an unusual amount. There were some small crafts from the surface, but we checked them out. Most of them went to tiny colonies where this guy would stick out like a sore thumb."

They always do give me the tough ones.

"Why'd they send you out anyway, his trail is probably cold by now."

"Well if he went off station he'd have to spend the same 3 weeks I did to get anywhere, and with the size of the payout, they're just assuming it's worth a little checking around. We've alerted people on some of the other stations to be on the lookout. When I heard about it I had a hunch, that if I was gonna do this job, I'd go to the surface."

"But the colonies are all farms, so how's he gonna spend that much cash down there? Maybe the bigger ones have some development but even then, all accounts with Earth go through the station and they would show up instantly."

"I'm not sure why, but my hunch is he's on the surface."

"Ok, well it's your time not mine you'll be wasting. I'll give you a list of the destinations and pilots of all the small craft that left that day and the surface to surface shuttles are pretty good. Have fun John, but don't say I didn't warn you."

I booked a shuttle down to Qurinius and went to my gate. The gate was done in a modern style with bench seats and a big Trans Mars Airways logo against the wall. The gate attendant wore the red and white uniform for the shuttle service. She started boarding 20 minutes after I got there.

As I boarded, I looked at the other passengers. The crowd consisted of some zealots in black and white suits with name plates, some beatniks, a few retired couples, some tourists, and a whole lot of colonial farmers. Quirinius was the largest colony and had shuttles to all the other settlements so it seemed like a good place to start.

The shuttle pushed off the station with thrusters and then completed the main engine burn to get it lined up for re-entry. The windows glowed for a short time and then you could see the big dome in the distance. We turned and headed toward its spaceport. I always hated martian landings, as they felt so strange to me, you fell both faster than slower than on Earth and it felt anything but good.

After being welcomed to Mars by the captain, I disembarked and headed for city hall. If there was any way I was going to find a needle in the haystack, it would only be with help from the colony administrator. I entered the modest office building resembling any glass tower on any planet, only scaled down due to the colony's size. My company informed them of my arrival. When I identified myself to the receptionist, I was sent right into the administrator's office.

"Mr. Delrio, good to see you come sit down."

"Administrator, thank you for your time."

"Mr. Delrio I'm pleased to meet with you to discuss this unfortunate, very unfortunate event. We here in the colonies like to keep to ourselves and keep the profits going off world to our landlords.

Any disruption of that flow causes all sorts of chaos down here. This thief has taken a critical shipment destined for the lead earthbound branch and this is totally unacceptable. I understand your company has insured the shipment, but the idea that we could lose a whole shipment is totally unacceptable."

"Is there anything you can tell me Administrator, either about the shipment or the thief?"

"It was a standard cash shipment, which we made as needed. When too much Earth currency builds up on the planet, we ship it back to Earth and the money is credited to our bank on arrival. Unfortunately, it is almost entirely untraceable as there's no uniformity of serial numbers, denominations, or even currencies. It's mostly what tourists have spent or families have brought that they either use to pay their surface taxes or buy trinkets from local shops. The money is then given to the central government for revenue. Any business on Mars is conducted in credits and so the cash becomes cumbersome and we ship it off world to the parent corporations. As for the thief, the only thing that I've heard is that he was dressed rather fashionably and that no one has seen him."

"I think he may have come back to Mars, Administrator, and I'm wondering if you have any idea where he could be?"

"Well the most lawless colony is Vulture Hollow on the Amazonian Plain, if you were ever going to find a terrorist like our thief you'll probably want to head there."

"Thank you Administrator, I'll give it a try."

As I left the building I noticed a space beatnik from my flight hanging out around the building. I headed toward the shuttle port and he followed me all the way, keeping his distance, but like an amateur who had never followed anyone before. He stood out like a sore thumb amongst the farmers with his beret and goatee. I booked a shuttle to Vulture Hollow and then walked toward the gate keeping an eye on the window. He followed me and bought a ticket immediately afterwards, but headed in a different direction.

    The crowd on the Vulture Hollow shuttle was a bit rougher, a large majority of them wore space biker club jackets for the Martian Marauders, a large club that roamed the rougher area of the planet. Word was they brought drugs in from offworld and were the main distributors on the planet. The rest of the people on the shuttle were younger than the average farmer and wore their party attire. The haze of cigarette smoke rose over the gate like a thick fog pressing down on my chest and I only imagined what the shuttle compartment would be like.

Inside the alcohol started flowing as soon as we took off. With the thick smoke, I even smelled marijuana. The flight lasted an hour and it ended with a rough landing.

Under its dome the town had one main road. It was lined with small casinos and bars, at the far end was an administrator's building which I walked to as quickly as I could. I witnessed two fistfights and countless street walkers. The administrator's building was almost empty with a secretary and one office, the rest of the building glowed with fluorescent lights and unused office space. I gave my name and company to the secretary. Almost immediately a balding overweight sweaty man ran out of the office.

"Mr. Delrio it's a pleasure to meet you, come in, come in."

"Administrator thank you for meeting me so-"

"Mr. Delrio it's my pleasure to do anything I can for you. We here love our offworld landlords and try to make them as much of a profit as possible. How can I help you?"

"Admini-"

"Call me Bobby Mr. Delrio."

"Ok, Bobby I was wondering if you could tell me anything about the robbery of that cash shipment that occurred a few weeks ago."

"Mr. Delrio I would love to help you but you're looking in a completely wrong direction. Somebody told you this was where all the trouble is and so you ran out here, I get it. But as administrator I know nothing about any of the workings of the casinos here. We believe that as long as people pay rent, taxes, and don't hurt government interests we leave them alone."

"Ok Bobby, but can you give me an idea of what someone would try to do to move all that cash."

"Well Mr. Delrio, anyone bringing that much cash to a casino would stick out like a sore thumb. What's more the casino wouldn't take it. Counterfeit money isn't usable for taxes, no matter how you get it, and if they thought it was the real shipment they'd just as soon turn them in. If not for the reward, then at least for the fact that we've been talking about banishment as the punishment for that crime at best."

"Banishment?"

"Oh yes Mr. Delrio's total inability to set foot under a corporate dome on Mars."

"Are there any other kinds?"

"Well there are the collectives."

"The collectives?"

"Yes sir, they make all their own goods."

"How do they survive?"

"It's a spare life Mr. Delrio, and they have to pay taxes like the rest of us but they have a different idea of how things should go."

"Communists?"

"No sir, I mean we all call them that, but they aren't associated with the Soviets, they hate the russians more than we do. No, they just like to share everything, some say that even includes their women. No it's one hundred percent collective, there's no representative body, they all make every decision."

"Young people?"

"Mostly but they have elders there too, it's a sight to behold."

"So nobody here would touch the cash, maybe we should look at it from the other angle, would anybody here have planned it?"

"Now if you're looking for that I may be able to help you out. The fact that those cash shipments happen is well known but which flight is a little bit of a secret. Only a few people in Quirinius know when the consolidated shipment occurs and they're either in the bank or the administrator's office."

"Say, that is a tip, thanks Bobby."

"Anything I can do to help Mr. Delrio, though you should stay a while and see what our town has to offer, there's some nice restaurants in the Sands."

"Maybe another time Bobby."

"Ok well good luck then Mr. Delrio."

I walked right back to the shuttle port, and booked a flight back to Qurinius. As I was waiting at the gate I saw the same beatnik staring at me from Qurinius. He looked to be just roaming around the airport. In a way it was a relief because it meant somebody had enough to hide that they'd go to the trouble of having me followed. I made a note next time I saw him to find out a little more about him.

Qurinius felt like a breath of fresh air compared to Vultures Hollow. There was a lot less smoking on the shuttle back. Mostly it looked like the day after the party in the shuttle cabin. People wore sunglasses and angry looks about the money they'd lost. It looked like I'd be here for a few days, so I booked a hotel. I made sure to get one with a bar, and a two and a half dollar steak at the hotel restaurant. That's where I went.

The bar was newly furnished with crystal globe light fixtures and orange upholstered seating. It was packed with customers. The hotel crowd consisted mostly of travelling businessmen with not a worn out father on vacation in sight. There were quite a few women in the bar as well. Some of them were on business thanks to women's lib. A few others looked like they were husband hunting. I settled down and ordered a Manhattan. I sat alone trying to puzzle out where I would go with that much cash. I started drawing ideas on a bar napkin as I sipped my drink. A woman walked up to me while I was lost in thought.

"Well hello, I've never met a millionaire before."

"What?"

"Well I mean you just keep scribbling dollar signs and lines; you must have a lot of money on your mind."

"Maybe I do, say I didn't catch your name."

"It's Emma, do you have a name?"

"Sorry excuse me, I was lost in thought, my name is John, how do you do?"

"Are you married, John?"

"Only to my work."

"How'd you like to buy a girl a drink?"

It didn't seem like a bad suggestion, so I ordered her a cosmo and we started talking. After a few minutes of niceties and flirting, the conversation turned to Mars

"You mean you don't live on the surface?"

"No, I'm from Earth, more specifically Cleveland. I'm just out here on business."

"Must be some business."

"Well what about you?"

"I'm a Martian girl through and through. I've spent my whole life on Mars, never left."

"Oh really? What would you do with a million bucks?"

"Get off world I guess."

"What if you wanted to stay?"

"Build a big house by the reservoir, just pay my rent and taxes, start a family, and make sure they have the best of everything."

"Did your family have a nice house?"

"My father was a miner in one of the deep mines. He was indentured since the company had paid for his ride to Mars. He met my mother here. After I was born, he skipped out on his servitude. They looked for him all over, but he took the whole family to Goldman's Rock where we worked on the commune. It was lovely there. I remember playing with all the other children. The work was hard, but everybody worked together. My mother and father liked it there very much. I grew up there. After my father succumbed to red lung, my mother just did the cooking in the community kitchen. Times got tough when rent was due. Eventually the commune couldn't pay anymore, so it disbanded. Most of the residents that could work went to Debbs Valley, but they wouldn't take any of the people with children. They were self-sustaining, but couldn't afford anyone that couldn't do a full day's work. I told my mother I was fine on my own and that she should go if they'd take her, which they did. I came back to Quirinius and took some business classes and got a job. Girls gotta pay the rent, and... That's my whole life story mister, I just get carried away when I talk about Goldman's".

"We have nothing like that back on Earth, at least not in the free world."

"It was an amazing experience, in some ways I'll always wish I could go back, but rocket your chin up as they say. So that's all about me, what about you, why do you have so much money on your mind."

"Oh, just a small thing, some offworld landlords lost some money on a business deal and they're having me chase after it."

"Simple as that huh?"

"Yeah I guess so... can I buy you another drink?"

"No I don't think so, one's my limit on a school night."

"Can I call you some time?"

She blushed slightly

"I guess you can John, my number is shield-5583. I think I'd like a call from you."

She walked off and I began to sip a second Manhattan in the hopes I'd fall asleep, the lower gravity meant you didn't press into bed as deeply, it was an odd feeling. I wrote down her number, sipped a third and even a fourth manhattan and then staggered to bed.

The next morning I woke up slightly hung over, showered, and turned on the radio. I went down to the hotel restaurant for breakfast and then headed to the Administrator's office. The receptionist buzzed the administrator, and this time he told her he was busy. I said I'd wait. After an hour the administrator looked out of his office, and seeing me a momentary cloud lowered over his face.

"Ah Mr. Delrio, so good to see you, sorry I've been so busy."

"That's alright Administrator, this won't take but a few minutes."

"That's fine Mr. Delrio, just fine, come right in."

I sat down across from the administrator, who was looking a little disturbed at the moment.

"So what can I do for you Mr. Delrio, did you have any luck in Vulture Hollow."

"Unfortunately no, Administrator, but they did bring up an interesting point there."

"And what is that Mr. Delrio?" His face soured as he said it.

"Well they said that only a few people know when the shipments go out and that they're either in your office or the central bank."

"I don't know what you're insinuating Mr. Delrio, but aside from myself there is only one other person in this office who knows when the monthly shipment goes out."

"And who would that be?"

"My most trusted aide, Marvin Edgeworth."

"Could I speak to Mr. Edgeworth?"

"I'm afraid not, you see he quit last week."

"Oh?"

"Yes, Marvin said he was having trouble with a relative and would have to leave to take care of them."

"And you didn't see anything strange about that?"

"Certainly not, Marvin was questioned by the authorities when the robbery happened and they found nothing suspicious. He had no unusual contact with anyone. Besides, Marvin has spent his whole life on Mars; there's nothing he would be willing to do to risk banishment."

"His whole life you say? Was he born in Quirinius?"

"No, Marvin came from a decidedly more plebeian background. For a while his family lived in one of the communal domes. This was before Marvin came to the city and made something of himself."

"I see, and who in the bank offices knew about the shipment."

"Why the president and whoever he trusts with the information? I have no idea."

"Thank you Administrator."

As I got up, he jumped up and half moved me along. Just before I reached the door, he looked at me in despair and almost pleadingly said, "You don't think Marvin had anything to do with it do you? I've known him since he just got out of junior college. He's been like a son to mc."

"I'm sure he wouldn't do anything wrong, Administrator. Maybe, I'll just ask him a few questions."

"Be careful if you go out to Debbs Valley Mr. Delrio. they're not too friendly towards outside authority."

"That's fine Administrator, I'll be just fine."

I went back to my hotel and had a vat grown hamburger, and then went up to my room. It was two in the afternoon and I had some time to kill. I put on a jazz station, and opened the bottle of whiskey I bought from the liquor store on the way home. I just sat there running over the details in my head, everything had been leading me to Debbs Valley, and yet I couldn't understand it. Would

Marvin risk his whole future just to live on some patch of desert under a second rate dome? And if so, who'd helped him? Why did nobody notice the cash coming from the station to some one horse colony in the middle of nowhere? It just didn't make any sense.

While I didn't have it all figured out yet, I did know what my next move was, and that required waiting till the afternoon. I sobered up by five, took a shower, and pressed my suit in the room. At six I picked up the phone and had the operator connect me to shield 5583.

"Hi Emma, it's John from the bar."

"Hello John, I was hoping you'd call."

"Emma, could I see you tonight, maybe we will have a nice dinner?"

"It's a little short notice, but I can get ready by seven, did you have any place in mind?"

"What's your favorite place to eat, star's the limit, it's on the company."

"Oh My, well I do like Ernie's by the spaceport, it's always nice to see the rockets."

"Should I pick you up?"

"No, I'll meet you there, just take a taxi."

"Alright seven at Ernie's it is."

I took a taxi out to the spaceport and saw Ernie's, I must've missed it when I landed. It was a well maintained building with huge plexiglass windows looking towards the spaceport. I arrived before Emma and asked for a table near the window. The place was busy but not full, and most of the people there looked like locals at a night out on the town. As I waited for Emma I saw the little space beatnik fellow who seemed to be following me. He walked up to the bar and sat down. Emma arrived soon afterwards. I got up. She smiled and blushed a little bit. She was wearing a simple dress, but it made her look good and she knew it. She had a look on her face like she had just been asked to prom. She sat down and we ordered some wine from the equatorial vineyards.

"You look very nice Emma."

"Why thank you John, I don't have a lot of occasions to get dressed up."

"That's a shame, but I'm sure happy to see you. How do you know about this place anyway?"

"Oh! All the locals know it. The food is decent, but the views are spectacular. Any time I want to have a special meal, I come here."

"Emma, can I ask you something?"

"Of course, anything John."

"Emma, do you know that short little fellow at the bar, the one with the beret?"

"No, I don't know many people in Qurinius I just know my boss Mr. Peterson and a few of my neighbors."

Playing a hunch I pressed her.

"Maybe not from Qurinius, maybe from a long time ago. How about when you were a child, maybe someone from Goldman's Peak?"

"Oh maybe, he sort of looks like little Carlo, but I haven't seen him in 10 years. It can't be him. What's this all about John?"

"Emma, remember when I said this meal was on the company?"

"Yes?"

"Well I'd like to ask you if you'd like to do some work for my company."

She wilted a little bit and said, "Oh, I thought this was a date."

"It is, Emma, but I think you can help me find that money my offworld landlords lost. I think it might have ended up in Debbs Valley and I was wondering if you'd take me out there. I hear they aren't too kind towards offworlders and I wonder if you'd be my guide. It might be a good chance for you to see your mother again."

"What would they need money for in Debbs Valley John?"

"I don't know, I was hoping you'd help me figure it out."

"Well I don't know how much help I can be about that."

"The company will pay you for your time and for transport to and from Debbs Valley. , Think of it as a paid vacation."

"Is that a vacation with you or are you more of a business traveller?"

"It's whatever you like Emma, I sure do like you, but the offer stands either way."

"Would you like to meet my Mother, John? I don't think I've ever had a date to meet my family."

It crushed me deep inside that she was so hopeful for someone to know her so quickly. There was a loneliness which I knew I would never be able to fill. I liked her, but it was about the job for me. I wasn't big on family, especially not a date's family. I dodged the question.

"Oh I don't know, I'm really interested in wrapping up this case I guess."

"Ok John, well let's have dinner and can I give you my answer tomorrow."

"Sure Emma."

We ordered two big steaks, and talked about Earth. I told her stories about what it was like to grow up there, and she sat enraptured, amazed at the technology and abundance that children in the free world had. I told her what it felt like to live under a blue sky, or how natural rain felt. She couldn't believe most of it, and looked at me doe eyed.

Dinner was over by nine and I took her out to the taxi stand and gave her my hotel number. I went back to the hotel, turned on the radio and tried to sleep. I couldn't help trying to figure out what all these connections meant, or if we'd find Marvin in Debbs Valley, or what was awaiting us out there. Around two am, I finally passed out and dreamt of tidal waves destroying island villages, and witch doctor's performing magical healings.

"I woke up to my phone ringing."

"Hello?"

"John? If the offer is still good I can take a few days off work and come with you. Mr. Peterson is nice enough to let me see my family again, he knows how rare the chance is."

"When can you leave?"

"As soon as you like."

"I'll check the shuttle schedule."

"Oh no, for Debbs Valley you have to charter a shuttle, or do surface transport, but that's 5 hours."

"Do you know anyone who would drive a shuttle out there?"

"One of the bush pilot's will usually do it."

"Ok I'll meet you down at the spaceport in half an hour."

I went down to the spaceport and asked for a shuttle pilot to Debbs Valley, most declined. Apparently, there was a rumor going around that they could collectivise your shuttle if you went there. Finally I found one that would. Rusty had a rough beard, and wore a heavily weathered leather bomber jacket. He had a Hughes cap on and showed me his shuttle, which he was exceptionally proud of.

"Sure I'll take you, is it a one way ride?"

"Actually I was hoping you'd wait around while we looked around for some time. Might be a couple days."

"I don't like hanging around all day, but my fee is fifty dollars a day, if you can pay that you can stay as long as you like."

I put a rocketgram through telling the company about the expense. When Emma arrived, I introduced her to Rusty and we got in the air. Rusty's shuttle was a tiny Hughes hyper fan four person craft that strained to get airborne in the thin air. We made it to Debbs Valley in half an hour.

When we landed, the station controller asked us our business in a stern tone. I got the feeling there were wrong answers to the question and said that we were taking Emma to see her family. He brightened up a little, and said that she lived in tower five. Rusty said he'd just as soon stay with the shuttle and handed me a communications earpiece, so I could call back to him. As we got out of the shuttle and went under the bubble, I noticed lots of people staring at us. I didn't exactly feel welcome. Under the dome, the city was ringed by settlement towers surrounding a public square. Beyond the settlement towers was the farmland and gardens. We walked up the hill to tower five and rang the buzzer for Emma's mother. An old woman answered.

"Yes Hello?"

"Mother, it's me Emma. I've come to visit and I brought a guest."

"Emma, is it really you? Come up, Come up."

We walked up three flights of steps and knocked on door 312. Emma's mother answered and was overcome with emotion. She didn't say anything at first. She just hugged her daughter tightly and then asked us both to come in.

"My darling, what brings you here?"

"I've come to visit Mother, just for a short while."

"How'd you get out here?"

"This man hired a shuttle, he says he has business out here and asked if I would bring him along."

Thunderclouds lowered over her mother's face and she looked at me with disgust

"If he's from the landlords, they'll get their rent soon enough."

"I'm not from the landlords, I work for an insurance company."

"Insurance, ha, won't nobody out here want any insurance."

"I'm not looking to sell, I'm looking for something that was insured, someone thought it might be out here."

She stared at me with a stone face, paused and then said "You should talk to Eugene. He speaks for all of us, but we defer to him for now. He'll be the man in robes under the tallest tree in the courtyard. Now Emma dear, you must tell me all about how you're doing. I want to know all about it."

I left the apartment and walked down to the courtyard. I found the tallest tree and under it was a man in green robes. When I walked up to him he smiled and asked "A challenge then?"

"I don't think so."

"You're not from around here, are you a stranger?"

"No."

"If you were I guess I would have known you already, what do you seek from a stranger?"

"Are you the leader here?"

"For now I guess."

"What do you mean for now?"

"Well I've been chosen to speak for the body for the moment, but I only hold the title as long as I resist all challenges with wisdom. I should say, there's no physical violence in Debbs valley."

"Well I was wondering if you know where I might find Marvin Edgeworth."

"Are you a friend of Marvin's Mr... Mr...?"

"Delrio."

"Mr. Delrio, oh I would guess you're not a friend of Marvin's then. I would guess you're from an offworld company."

"Do you know where Marvin is?"

Eugene paused, and then after a minute said "I tell you what Mr. Delrio, I will show you where Marvin is tonight, until that time why don't you have some refreshments in our bar. "

He pointed towards a building all the way at the end of the ring far away from the plaza. I walked off, and by the time I got to the bar a bell was ringing. Tenor so young people walked out just as I walked in. Inside were a few young men and women and a bartender with a rugged face.

"Mr. Delrio, have a seat, we don't have a menu but our kitchen is mighty fine, can I interest you in anything?"

"How did you know my name?"

"Oh well, Eugene sent an electric message ahead. We don't normally serve strangers but he said to make an exception for you."

"Can I get a hamburger?"

"Sure Mr. Delrio, anything else you want."

"How about a beer?"

"We have our own beers here, brewed on site. They're pretty tasty, though I haven't had non communal beer in 40 years."

"What do I owe you?"

"Oh we don't take money Mr. Delrio, to each and from each as it were?"

"To each and from each?"

"To each according to need and from each according to ability."

"So you are communists."

"No Mr. Delrio, we do share our belongings but we're not Reds. We hate the Soviets just as much as you do. No, we live here as collectivists. Let me get your food and I'd be more than happy to tell you about it."

He poured me a beer and walked off. As I looked around, younger patrons were mostly drinking milkshakes, and reading from what appeared to be textbooks. One man at a table pointed at me and lowered his voice, while the women at his table giggled.

The bartender returned with my food in 10 minutes and refilled my beer. I took a bite out of the burger and then asked him "So what's a collectivist then"

"Well we make all decisions as a group, every decision is voted on by the entire community if it's important enough. Eugene guides the process and makes suggestions, but we also allow anyone in the community to make suggestions as well. We have sub councils for smaller specialized decisions. Eugene sort of acts as our voice when there's no time to ask everyone. However, everyone including Eugene is picked by the entire community."

"What about money, or possessions?"

"Everyone is given a place to live and a job, and as much food as they want. No place to live is nicer than any other. Unless you have children, then you get a family sized unit. We can have whatever possessions we like. When you pass on, all possessions save for a few personal ones return to the collective. Everyone is given a small wage for outside spending along with their daily bread."

"Their daily bread?"

"That's what we call food, clothing, medicine, and shelter, all your needs are met by the collective and you're then given a small wage for out of colony purchases."

"People don't buy things in the colony?"

"Why would you, everything is provided for in the most pleasant way possible."

"I sipped on the beer, which was quite good, and finished my hamburger."

"Can you put a game on or something?"

"We have some old kinetoscopes that get broadcast throughout the colony, I can turn that on."

"That's fine."

I got lost in the TV drama on TV, it was a Playhouse 90 production of The Master Builder, the lead was engrossing as a single minded man of vision. After the show was over, it went right into a production of Rebecca for TV. I was starting to get interested when the bartender came up to me.

"They're ready for you now Mr. Delrio."

"They?"

"Just go on down to where you met Eugene and you'll find everything you're looking for."

I walked out the door and was shocked. The whole colony was assembled in the green in the center. Eugene stood on a stage with a microphone. Beside him was the beatnik who i'd seen following me and another boyish looking man in new clothes.

"Come down Mr. Delrio, as I promised Marvin is here, I'm sure you have some questions for him."

I walked down through the crowd, and saw the second thing that threw me for a loop. In the center of the crowd was a giant pile of cash, as big as the missing shipment. I walked up to the stage, and they pinned a microphone on my lapel.

"Mr. Delrio, this is Marvin. As you've already guessed, Marvin was the one who told us when the shipment was scheduled to leave. Marvin and Carlo have told us that you're an insurance investigator, and that you're here to try and prevent your offworld company from insuring the shipment. You're not the police, and so your only interest is recovering that giant pile of money in the midst of our colony. Is that correct?"

"Yes, that's correct" I mumbled, I was dumbstruck.

"Then watch what we have decided to do."

At that moment several men in the crowd poured what must have been fuel over the money and then lit it ablaze.

"But why?"

"Mr. Delrio, this colony owes its landlord and was about to be reclaimed. Some of us came from Goldman's Peak and remembered what the separation was like the last time a colony was reclaimed. Marvin remembered, and we as a colony decided to reclaim assets from the offworlders by taking that shipment. Now that you are here, searching for Marvin, it would only be a matter of time. Rather than give the offworlders the satisfaction of recovering their money, or leaving poor Marvin to suffer alone, we have decided to burn this shipment. You and your pilot will be held until morning. By then the colony will have disbanded, scattered to the four winds."

I watched that expensive bonfire burn as they tied me up. I saw them push Rusty up on the stage with me and tie him up as well. Everyone began to disperse to ships at the port. Suddenly there was a face I recognized walking towards us. Emma came up to me.

"Hi John."

"Hi Emma."

"I don't think either of us expected for it to end up this way."

"I don't think so either."

"I'm going to leave with the other colonists. A group of us from Goldman's Peak are all going together. It's one of the things I've hoped for all of my life, to be with my family again."

"I hope it works out Emma."

"What will you do, will you send them to chase us down?"

"No, Eugene was right, I was sent to recover the money. Now that it's gone, that's the end of my interests. Other than telling the authorities what happened my business is done here. I'm not even sure the authorities will chase them down as you've all already banished yourselves."

"Well I guess this is goodbye then John."

"Goodbye Emma."

She walked away with a group of twenty-somethings towards the spaceport laughing and hugging them as she went.

Advanced Rocketry

Ares Towers were the newest construction in Quirinius, and they towered over the city, letting their residents survey Mars at their feet. Robert Carr stood on the 45th floor in his oversized apartment wondering which woman he would see tonight. He was tall, fit, and in his late twenties. He wore a full black suit with a thin tie. The club x15 had prepared a dinner of Japanese style beef and Maine style lobster, all locally grown in martian cloning farms, and had sent the meal up to his apartment. His date for the evening, Elaina, looked beautiful, but her moods made her seem like two people. They alternated between boundless material avarice and the certainty of a world weary equal. He had been dating her for nearly three months. He first caught a glimpse of her at a fashion show mixer and won her interest with his talk of the discoveries he was on the cusp of at Hughes. She had been a model, but was now a fashion buyer's agent, and she made it her business never to miss a prize. The doorman called up and Robert had him escort her to the maglev elevator, he put a Martian samba optical tape on and opened the door before she knocked.

Elaina wore a figure fitting sleeveless green dress which landed well above the knee with trendy, cheap plastic. Her heels added a full three inches to her height and made her slightly taller than him.

"I'm just simply exhausted darling, I've had such a full day. It's such a treat to see you," Elaina remarked.

"As always it's nice to see such a beautiful woman walk into my apartment."

"Darling, can you believe it? I had to fight for a dress from a designer with another bidder." Normally the other bidders dropped out when they heard they were competing with Elaina's boss, Steven Lord. When she had to compete for anything, it always vexed her as if the concept of competition itself was novel.

"Darling, they drove the price up twelve hundred dollars," she added. "Steven was so furious, he contacted all the other designers he knew and made sure they would never sell to this person again."

"Who was it?"

"That's the thing, it was some off-world buyer who had seen the dress in a newsreel. I don't know who they were but whatever country they came from they must be pretty important there."

Robert tried his best to be empathetic, "I'm so sorry, Elaina. Cigarette?"

"Oh I've had the most wonderful Cigarettes, they're from the eastern colonies, they're supposed to be like french ones, but better of course."

"Do you have any?"

"Just one and I was saving it for myself, unless..." and here her eyes became wide and she put on a look that was a mature version of whining, "Unless you could have the doorman get some more, they're terribly expensive I'm afraid." Robert suggested, "I'll send down for some and we'll have them by the end of dinner."

He buzzed the doorman and then they proceeded to eat the japanese style beef.

Elaina ate complacently, always repeating the phrase "Can you believe there's someone who would go against Steven"

Robert was pretty sure after dinner she'd be staying over, she had left her toothbrush at his apartment within a month, by three she had not only casual clothes but an ensemble fit for breakfast. She rarely stayed past breakfast unless they were going shopping, but she usually liked to dress up if they were going to shop downtown.

The doorman knocked just as they were finishing the lobster. She had made several suggestive motions with her mouth around the shellfish during dinner so he was pretty certain of how things would proceed. He took the carton from the doorman and tipped him twenty dollars, then opened it with a knife and took out two packs.

"These are quite good, almost a chocolate flavor," he said.

"Yes I know darling that's why I had to have them."He put an optical tape from Sarah Vaughn and after another cigarette they went to bed.

"It won't work Mr. Carr" said Severius. "And why is that? Have you made an alteration."

"Nnno Sir, No alterations," Severius whimpered.

"Then according to Altman's laws this engine should be 30% more powerful."

"Iiiit's not a matter of more powerful Mr. Carr, it just won't work," Severius explained.

"What do you mean won't work, it's a standard rocket with a few changes in the de Laval nozzle, following Altman's laws" Robert retorted.

"Bbbbut Mr. Carr the problem is with the design, it keeps blowing up, when we do get it to fire it's grossly over expanded and a shockwave forms. It's a bad design."

As soon as Severius said this, the look on his face made it clear he wished he could grab the last sentence and shove it back into his mouth. He continued trying to correct himself. "Not that you haven't followed Altman's laws exactly as they've been laid out, your implementation should be more powerful. Absolutely Mr. Carr, it's just that there seems to be a problem with this particular design."

"Severius, I'm sure you've overlooked something in your implementation, do you want me to look for another more senior member for your team?"

All the blood ran out of Severius' face, and what had been whimpering became a quiet defeated resolve.

"Nnnno Mr. Carr, I'm sure I've made a mistake, I'll fabricate another engine according to the design, I'm sure I'll get it to work this time."

"Feel free to stop by again if you have any trouble with the fabrication process. I'm not an expert in fabrication, but I'm sure I can provide some help."

"Ooof course Mr. Carr, thank you, Severius replied.

Carr wondered why Severius never seemed to follow directions the first time. He always had to be prodded or cajoled. When there was a real issue, Carr could resolve it within seconds, yet Severius had to be encouraged to the point where the issue would present itself. Carr had done four previous rocket designs before this one, each for a different purpose or optimization, but each, as long as it had followed Altman's laws and had been in conformance with current methodologies, had been a big success. Carr was a smart man but he wasn't, as he would say, some egghead from the university. Instead he followed the latest trends coming out of industry and the academy, then simply implemented the principles proposed. This extended well beyond rocket design, as a team leader he followed the latest trends in technical project management and implemented them, or at least conformed to them in some fashion. Whatever he did, he was at least better than Millsky, that alone made him the star of the department.

"Mr. Carr, call on line one" said his secretary.

"Who is it Janet?"

"It's Mr. Asheton Bremerwood," she responded.

"I'll take it"

Robert picked up the phone,"Ash, how are you"

"Pretty good Bobby, and you?"

"Doing well as always"

"Bobby, I'm in Quirinius for a few days. Do you want to get dinner and drinks tonight and see if we can raise a little hell?"

"I don't have any plans tonight? Any place you wanna try?"

"How about Katakana I hear their sushi is amazing"

"Sure Ash, you're the boss"

"Looking forward to it Bobby, I'll see you at the bar around six"

"Sounds good Ash, see you then"

Robert hung up and turned to Janet. He asked, "Janet, do I have anything this evening?"

"There was the lecture at Edgeworth University on new technologies"

"Call Dr. Abatan and have him send over the relevant papers, and then call Martin Orlof and say I won't be able to make it tonight"

"Yes Mr. Carr," Janet affirmed.

Drinks at six meant that Ash would be there at six fifteen which gave him enough time to go home and put on a more casual suit. Drinking with Ash usually meant drinking too much, and then usually chasing whatever secretary was left in the bar by the time Ash had had enough. Elaina only stopped by when they had plans, though he resolved tonight that, not for fidelity, but for his own standards, he'd only bring home a beautiful woman, as there had been enough refuse in his past. He got to Katakana at six twenty five, having taken a cab from his apartment after a change and shower. Ash was there with a drink ready for him.

"Bobby good to see you"

"As always the same Ash, how's Hawthorne?"

"Same stuffy old city, when was the last time you went back to Styler to see anyone"

"I don't go back often enough, it's a 30 minute maglev ride, I should go more often, but even after the maglev, then you have to navigate out to Oxfordtown to get there. The campus is so insular."

"Talliper asked about you last time I was there"

"Old Talliper, is he still giving the undergraduates the scare of their life on fuel mixtures"

"The same exams even. I also saw Professor Shaw"

"Did he ask about me?"

"Actually he did Bobby, he asked whether you had 'straightened out'"

"HA, that old stick in the mud is the same as ever. So Ash, what brings you down here besides chasing some poor secretary around the bar?"

"Big stuff Bobby, my think tank sent me down here to track the future of rocketry, and your name came up a few times to say the least."

"What would that mean, Ash?"

"Bobby, it might mean Solar System level recognition, I know you've done a few designs, but it might mean enough credentials to start your own company. Investors follow our papers very closely"

"You think so Ash?"

"Bobby they sent me down to talk to you about what you're up to"

"That's the whole reason you're down here"

"Well you and one other guy, an Irwin Millsky, he works at your company"

"What could they possibly want with Millsky"

"Well word is Bobby he's produced some counter intuitive designs. They want me to look at them and see if they make any sense."

"Counter Intuitive is polite, his garbage always under performs"

"The better for you Bobby, now let's get some food in our stomachs before we find some companionship"

The sushi was passable, both men had ample orders of the vat grown uni along with a wide assortment of fish selected by the chef. After dinner Robert led them to an upscale tiki bar on the ground floor of the Bellman Hotel. The men were over dressed compared to the rest of the patrons, but their suits exuded money. Asheton took some coca out of his pocket and they each did a line. The coca had the desired effect as a few minutes later two women came over to their Tiki Hut and asked if they could join the party. They took separate cabs home, Asheton and Vanessa in one, Robert and Amy in the other, though no names would be remembered the next day. The girls' apartments were downtown.

Amy lived in a first colony condo that belonged to her aunt and was still under rent control. Vanessa's was new construction a few blocks away. At Amy's apartment they snorted a few more lines of coca and then went into her bedroom.

Both men were finished with their woman after an hour and flagged cabs to take them home.

On the cab ride home Robert wondered what Millsky could have possibly done to spark the interest of anyone.

Millsky was a sloppy dishevelled individual. He always had stains on his button down or tie. His slightly overweight stature was topped off with a bird's nest for hair. He kept trimmed in a crew cut until things got busy and then he would let it grow too long. His designs always under-performed Carr's by twenty to thirty percent, and were, if not haphazard, at least not measured. Like a Jackson Pollock painting Millsky would make a design that he felt would work in one big leap and then constantly revise it to get the performance numbers necessary. Sometimes he would scrap his designs entirely and try a second approach. Carr hated him with a passion, especially his sloppiness, his weak methodologies. Rumor has it that Milksky was hired because he was cheap, even though he had been working on rockets for twenty years.

Carr was a little hung over the next day, but by 10, after a cup of coffee, he had leveled out. Dr. Abermoff came by his office.

"Bob, do you have a minute?"

"Of course Dr. Abermoff, is everything ok?"

"Fine fine, listen I'm sure as you already know, Asheton Bremerwood is here from the Lloyd Group."

"Ash and I had dinner last night."

"Fantastic, so you know why he's here"

"We didn't go too deep into it, but he said he wanted to review my work and Millsky's to understand the future of rocketry."

"That's my understanding as well, and I know you're going to go all out letting your work shine. But I'd like you to stand up for Millsky as well. We want the whole company to look good, not just you. It'd mean a lot if you could help Millsky put his best foot forward. Some of his designs are really pretty interesting, and while he doesn't get the performance that yours do, they have innovative uses."

"Well I have no idea what he's working on"

"Go down to his lab, I'll let him know that he's to show you his work. I want you two to work as a team for Bremerwood, so that the company, and not just you, benefit from this report. There's plenty of limelight to go around and I'm sure you'll come out smelling like a rose, but just think of the company for a little bit."

"Of course Dr. Abermoff"

Millsky's lab was a mess with tubing and exhaust scoring all over. He had three technicians working for him, all of them were offworlders who spoke broken English. Milsky sat at a desk in the lab, papers, and an old hyperterminal covering his desk, along with some more tubing.

"Mr. Carr, good to see you, what brings you down here."He adjusted his tie and brushed some carbon dust off of his blue button down shirt.

"Dr. Abermoff said that I should come down and look at your work, so that we could present the work of the company better to Mr. Bremerwood."

"Of course, Of course. And you know Bremerwood already"

"Asheton and I went to school together yes"

"Dr. Abermoff sent me the memo electronically on the new xerox alto system letting me know the details."

"Oh"

Millsky was obsessed with the gadgetry of computers. Three weeks ago he had asked all of us to only send him memos electronically. The secretaries all had the system but they hated typing it twice.

"So I'll show you my latest creation then." Millsky was always direct; he was awkward at best with small talk and was terrible to get a drink with.

"Ok"

"This is a regular type 99 C rocket engine with a 3 percent growth in thrust as the target. The only modification from the type 99 c is a small indentation in the side of the nozzle and fuel use is exactly the same."

"But Altman's laws state that any increase of thrust must increase fuel," Robert remarked.

"I've found Altman's laws to break down about 2 percent over the type 99, experimentally when I tried to go much higher. Surely you've run into that with your new engine? 30 percent greater than your last one puts you at about 8 percent over the type 99. You've been getting over …. "

"I haven't read anything about this in the literature."

"It's a small community, there was an earthside researcher who was running into the issue and sent out a request on a mailing list that the xerox alto got. He's from Taiwan and it was a Chinese language list, but Xen Ding was subscribed. We corresponded and he also…"

"So this is some Red Chinese design"

"No no no, Taiwan, it's the government in exile."

"Has this researcher published?"

"No he's still working out the details, we may have a paper in the fall depending on how things go"

"Can I see the nozzle"

"Sure"

Millsky walked over to a blasting chamber and turned the nozzle towards Carr, covering his hands with soot. Carr was careful not to touch anything.

"You see the groove has to be about 80 percent up the nozzle, the exact height isn't known yet for optimal efficiency"

Carr studied the indentation for a few seconds.

"Well thank you Mr. Millsky, this will be most helpful, I'm sure Ashe will love it."

"Any time Mr. Carr."

Carr went to his office as if on a mission and had his secretary immediately call in Severius.

"Severius, I have a new idea I'd like you to try, can you put a groove 80 percent up in the nozzle on the fabrication you're going to do tonight."

"MMMMister Carr, we weren't going to do one tonight, we just fabricated," Severius protested.

"So in that case can you do one tonight with the modification I specified?"

"OOOOf course MMMMister Carr."

"And can it be ready and tested by tomorrow?"

"WWWee'll have to work the night but yyyees!"

"This is a fire drill Severius, so get to it, I'll be accessible via phone at my apartment."

It was just like Millsky to go with second rate science, but if it worked it worked, and it'd be able to solve his problem. He'd have something impressive to show Ashe tomorrow and the company would look good for all of it.

Carr went home and ordered delivery from the local Italian restaurant. At 11:45 his phone rang.

"Hello"

"YYYYYEsss Mr. Carr, we've fashioned it and done the usual testing and it appears to work."

"Fantastic Severius, now everybody will need to be there by 9:30 tomorrow for Mr. Bremerwood"

"YYYYEss Mr. Carr."

"Good Night Severius, and great work, I'll remember this."

"YYYESss Mr. Carr."

At 9:00 Dr. Abermoff called Millsky and Carr into a conference room where they both went over their current work, neither mentioned the groove in the nozzle specifically but both presented results beyond the point that Altman's Laws broke down. Asheton repeatedly asked about their performance levels, and after hearing Carr's higher than Millsky, he seemed to settle in. There were pastries and coffee and after each having one and a cup of coffee, Asheton asked to see a test firing of Carr's engine. Carr agreed showing no hesitation, but inwardly felt somewhat nervous. Dr. Abermoff had Carr call in Severius and arrange the firing. They all went out to the lab.

"Everything ready, Severius?" Carr asked.

"YYYYEESssss Mr. Carr, all set"

"Let's go then"

Severius pressed the button and the room lit up as they all observed the rocket in the chamber.

"Current thrust level Severius?" Carr asked

"AAAAte percent over a type 99"

"Ok let's shut it down"

"YYESSss Mr. Carr"

Bremerwood patted Carr on the back "Carr that's amazing, let's get drinks tonight"

"Sure Ashe"

Dr. Abermoff asked Asheton if he wanted to see Millsky's as well.

"No no, that won't be necessary, you've both done amazing work, Rocketdyne is where the stars go to shine apparently. I'm very impressed and will say as much in the report, you guys are upper right quadrant material."

Dr. Abermoff suggested a steakhouse for lunch. Then Millsky, Carr, Bremerwood and himself left the offices. They each had one drink for lunch and all except Millsky left to go home.

Millsky returned to the lab to check his design. Carr went home and freshened up for another evening with Bremerwood. Bremerwood went to the hotel and did the same. They met at a Martini bar close to Bremerwood's hotel.

"Bobby, my report will take a couple of weeks before you see it, but while I'm going to make a glowing recommendation for Rocketdyne, I'm going to mention you by name. At the Lloyd group we knew Altman's laws broke down at a few percent over the type 99, but the second breakdown at 7 percent of all our fixes is what really stumped us. And unless you fabricated last night, you seem to have solved that Bobby, as we've found any rocket over a few days old would blow up with the fix we've seen. Bobby, this report wasn't out of the blue. A small group of investors wanted to burst scale a new rocket company, and they were looking for a head of engineering. They had talked about acquiring Rocketdyne, but Millsky is only doing the work that's already somewhat known. You've taken it to the next level. When I name you in the report, that should be enough accolade along with your history to make you a shoe in. I'd be leaving the Lloyd group as well. These guys have deep pockets, they've talked about making me CEO because of my connections. What do you say Bobby are you in?" Without a second of consideration Carr replied, "Of course Ashe, it sounds amazing."

Rocket Bodhisattva

On the steps of the Columbia library, I smoked a joint, looked up to the sky and felt its call. I had been in the merchant marines during the war. Lying about my age, I stayed in until 48, after which I bounced around from coast to coast. I had been a farm worker, a waiter, a train conductor, a truck driver, and worked in a newspaper print shop. When Ike's guys landed on the moon, I went back to school on the GI bill trying to be some sort of writer. I met Carlo at Columbia and we fell in fast. We would go out to his mother's place in Jersey and then to the falls, smoke a joint, and watch the stars rotate through the sky. He called them a dynamo, but I longed to see the Earth from the other side. I wanted to see it spinning like Eames' tops. From my years passing from east to west, I'd met a few characters, a Salt Lake City drunk, a San Franciscan Chaucer, anarchists and fascists, perverts and pious. And I had seen the states as only a hobo can. Now the moon called to me, and beyond, the new Venusian horizons, taunted by that brightest of shining stars in the morning sky. The ancient pagan atua of Venus haunted my dreams, begging me to worship them. At Columbia I was much older than my classmates, but fell in with a few freaks, including Harold whose father was a high diplomat at the UN. Harold's father had met the Venusian envoy. When regular saucer flights from the moon's space station started travelling to Venus, he had been one of the first to go. At first carrying Ike's good wishes, then later when Kennedy had kept him on he had gone back again. Prof. Walters had vouched that I would be a solid hire once I had completed the program to *Life Magazine*. I asked if I could do an assignment on travelling in the new era, to the colonies on the moon and seeing what the new world of the Venusians could tell us. They had sent photographers when things had first opened up, and a camera crew had even shot a film that played around theaters. The films showed the industrial fervor of building out the moon colonies, and the beauty of the Venusian Idols surrounding their thatched homes with their scantily clad women. When I tried to sell my assignment, I told stories of how I'd bummed around, described my journals from that time, and how I'd like to do a journal of bumming around in the new space age. To my amazement, and I think due to Walters' pull, they went for it. Wild Man, Wild.

I stood at the base of the Queensboro Bridge and hitched a ride out to the Montauk Spaceport. When I arrived, they checked my ticket, and press credentials, and let me sit at the gate. With space travel off of Earth you had to show up at least 5 hours early. Once you were up there though, it was like catching any other airline flight. The Trans Galaxy rocket sat on it's pad going through checkout. There were daily flights from Montauk to the station, but flights from Earth station to moon station only went three times a week. Moon station to Venus was a daily saucer flight as the moon colony traded frequently with them. Sitting around me were all kinds: businessmen and union tradesmen. The station was constantly expanding and new ship construction happened in a drydock at its far end. Some guy was reading a paper and I asked him if I could have a section. There was a news item about Richard Burton and Liz Taylor's followup to Cleopatra, and a woman in her underwear selling "high fashion". I asked him what he was going up through the stratosphere for.

"I got a job managing one of the restaurants in the old wing of the station"

"Fancy place?"

"Nah, but people gotta eat somewhere, it can't all be tubes and straws"

"You've been up there before man?"

"Only once, my wife and I got a day trip from our relatives for our honeymoon. It was before the gravity inducers were put in. We stayed in a hotel for one night and floated all around. It's different now, you feel like you're planet side."

"Far out."

"What are you going for?"

"I'm gonna write an article about travelling for *Life Magazine* about space travel and what it's like to go to Venus."

"Venus? Why would you wanna go there? Those people are crazy. They pray to idols and you can't get a decent meal to save your life. It's just odd fruits and vegetables, and occasionally some sort of Venusian fish that is bitter."

"You been there man?"

"Nah, I just read the articles. I watched the movie when it was in theaters too, and on my honeymoon they had a Venusian meal shipped in."

"I wanna see it for myself man, see the whole wild planet."

"Good luck buddy. If you want a real meal, stop by Ernie's in the station before you go."

"Maybe I'll take a short trip to Rio there man."

"The rocket flights to South America are at the new extension on the other end."

"Crazy man."

The square started looking through me in another direction and I kept paging through the few sheets of newspaper he had passed along. A chicken with a tourniquet on her finger in a stewardess outfit came out and announced boarding, and we all lined up. As we boarded she ripped our tickets, and told us our seats.

I walked onto the boarding platform and looked at the sky as the elevator started moving. We got to about three quarters up the side, and walked through the open door.

For Earth to station Trans Galaxies, the seating areas were a series of spheres stacked vertically, each with its own door. Inside each sphere were rows of seats when it was time to launch the spheres rotated so our backs were to the ground and then blast off.

Everybody boarded and the stewardesses checked all our belts, shut the door, and then buckled in themselves. The pilot came over the loudspeaker.

"Ok folks, we're set to have a short flight of about two hours to rendezvous with the station. Stewardesses prepare for rotation."

The whole world turned and suddenly we were all lying down on our backs. They did the countdown over the speakers and when it hit zero I felt an off the wall a-bomb hit my chest. The pressure kept building for about two minutes after which, everything got back to normal for a little bit. Then an even bigger a-bomb hit my chest for a minute, and suddenly I was floating in the sky with the stars. For short flights like this, they didn't add the weight of gravity inducers to the rockets, to save fuel, so you got to float like a comet until you hit the station. My belt pulled against my chest and I just wanted to float away. My pocket change rattled around in my pocket floating as the ship moved up and down. We all just sat strapped into our seats. Trans Galaxy was the top as they had headphones in the front pocket for everyone in little plastic bags. I took the set out of the seatback in front of me, opened it, and plugged it into the armrest. There were 4 channels, a classical program, a tourist news show about Earth station, a jazz station, and a pop station. I listened to the tourist program. They talked about hotels on the station, restaurants, zero g attractions, and connecting flights.

As I was learning how to be a cube in space, I suddenly pressed against my belt, and then the rocket smashed against some other metal surface. The pilot broke in over the audio and said "OK folks, that's the end of this flight. Welcome to Earth station." We sat still for a little bit and there was a buzzing from outside the door. All of a sudden, I sank in my chair like a brick, then the stewardess came over the loudspeaker. She told us we could all unbuckle. The door abruptly opened there was an audible whoosh of air. We all filed out the door and down the corridor to a row of men sitting at little cubes with gates beside each one. As each person filed through, the man at the desk asked if they had anything to declare. When it was my turn in front of the line, I said "My own genius, Wilde man Wilde." The customs agent smirked and told me to move along. The hallways were all metal with high ceilings. It was hard to figure out the shape of the station itself. They always kept adding to it, and as far as I knew, it was about 10 city blocks worth of offices, storefronts, embassies, restaurants and hotels, with extra room for the docks, and mechanicals. I walked down to the departure board, and saw the next moon station flight wasn't until tomorrow. I'd have to spend the night in the station. I didn't want to book a hotel and wanted to check out the pulse of the place, so I decided I'd get a good meal and then crash on the floor. I had a thick jacket that would be pretty warm, and the climate control felt like 70 or so.

I spotted the guy from the spaceport lobby, and followed him down through the station. He walked all the way to the end and there in neon. It was Ernie's. I saw him walk up to another guy in a tie. They shook hands and the other guy left. I sat on the floor and waited about forty five minutes, watching people go by, smoking a cigarette here and there. At about ten minutes to nine east coast time I walked in. He saw me, and winced a little. I walked up to the counter and said "Hey man, you think I could get some grub on the house?" He winced again, looked at the serving window and saw a dead plate from a diner that was left. It must've been baking under the window for a while, as the bun was a little tough. He handed it over and a cup of coffee without saying much.

After dinner I sat on the stone walkway, and watched people walking by. At about Twelve eastern I made a trip to the drug store and bought a pack of Lucky's and a bottle of gin. The foot traffic slowed down as it got to mid day Moscow time and I found a doorway for maintenance where I could huddle up. I drank the gin quickly and passed out. The next few hours I woke up once or twice seeing more foot traffic consisting of Asian people, and then passing out again. I had a vision of a giant altar with smoke coming from it. I was standing in front of it with a beautiful Venusian woman beside me and surrounded by Venusians chanting. The statue of a giant atua was in front of us and on the altar were all kinds of strange foods.

I woke up around 6 a.m. eastern and went to Ernie's again. The manager was still there, he saw me and handed me another dead plate, this time overcooked chipped beef. He gave me a coffee and said from now on no more freeloading. The chipped beef had formed a skin and was a little tough to choke down but felt warm in my stomach. I was still a little drunk and had a few hours to kill so I went down to the American Express office and checked if Life had left me any messages. Zippo. I sat in the lounge and watched all the squares come in and out doing business, sending messages, and asking to use the phone. Occasionally a young couple would come in and check their messages. They always seemed hopeful. The guy behind the desk sat there pleasantly answering all the requests. After a while he started staring at me, I think he'd smelled the alcohol on my breath when I went up there. At some point he walked over to another guy and whispered to him and pointed at me. I beat it out of there and walked down to the docks. It was almost time to board my flight anyway. For Earth station to moon station flights you didn't have to wait as long before boarding. The crowd seemed a lot more rugged for this trip. If I'd been a whaling man last time around this is the crew I think I'd see. There were a few squares in nice suits, but most of the guys were workmen for the moonbase. Smoke hung in the air and there was a low rumble. A few of the guys were reading comic books, or cheap pulps. The stewardess looked more like an old barmaid in a uniform than the last trip. An hour before launch we all boarded, no rotating chambers this time. We all buckled in and waited. They never had safety announcements on these flights because if something happened you were just a goner. There was a thud as the ramps pulled back, and then we all heard little buzzes as the thrusters pushed us away from the station. This took maybe ten minutes, and then everything was very still. Zonk!!! All of sudden I was slammed back in my seat! I felt like I was five hundred pounds. After about five minutes it let up. The Earth station moon station shuttle had a gravity inducer so when the captain told us we could get up, I walked over to the lounge. The gin was starting to wear off and I just wanted to have another drink. Some of the other passengers were talking about the work on the moon base.

"That's what I'm sayin' mack. Under the dome with the fake gravity it's just like any other construction job. Lumbers lumber, bricks, brick, and steels, steel. Pay's just a lot better."

"What about outside the dome?"

"That's the tough stuff since sometimes it's in low g. If they cover it with gravity, then the suit weighs a ton. But that pays the most."

I thought of the line in the Isha Upanishad about the self holding the cosmos together and wondered what the holy books of the Venusians said. Nobody had translated or published them earthside, and while the Venusians had advanced technology they lived like stone age man. They had welcomed the ambassadors with open arms, and saw us as a curiosity. The Soviets didn't bother with them as much, but would occasionally hold them up as models of communal living.

I went back to my seat and fell asleep for a while. When I woke up, we were an hour from Moon Station. I pulled the headphones from the seat back and plugged in, they had the Steve Allen show on a screen in front of the seating area. I just stared and let the time pass by. All of a sudden the pilot told us to buckle up. I pressed against the belt for a little and then a loud thud. I heard the walkway line up and they unsealed the door. Everybody drowsily stood up and rambled out. I walked out past customs and after checking the map looked for the Venusian docks.

  The Venusians had built the entrance to their own gangway as a sort of cultural exchange. It was made out of large pieces of smooth rock with round pieces of a metal I'd never seen before holding it together. A small roof was fashioned over the desk from blue wood and the floor was covered with a reddish grass. As I walked up a Venusian started speaking to me. The Venusians spoke with their minds, and you heard when they were talking to you was a genderless neutral voice in your head, almost like interviewing your brains. While they could send voices to you, you still had to speak with them.

"Hello Mr. Beaumont, your saucer will leave in han hour or so, please be seated"

"How did you know who I was?" I asked.

"While we know many things Mr. Beaumont you are the only non Venusian on this trip and your magazine faxed your picture ahead when asking for travel permission."

"Oh, Thanks"

I sat and looked around at the other Venusians. Most wore smooth fabric tunics, but there were a few whose clothes looked like it was made from a purple animal skin. Most of them stared into the distance, one or two looked at each other, occasionally one would have a facial reaction for no reason. They must've been chatting up a storm.

Venusians looked mostly like humans except they had green skin, blue hair, and purple eyes. Some of the women wore necklaces with red stones cut in a series of squares or rectangles tied together with blue fibers.

All of a sudden every Venusian stood up and walked over to the gate, I got in line with them. We all walked down the gangway and suddenly I was inside a saucer.

Images of an Island

Frank always thought, "No matter how bad it gets, the one thing they can't take from you is the refuge of imagination." Frank imagined himself to be in different places all the time, but the one he always returned to like a crutch was Hawaii. It was the main reason he had gotten into his line of work and why he was able to make any kind of living doing it.

Frank hadn't sold a tiki remodel in over three weeks and times were getting a little desperate.

"It's about being somewhere else," he told the Bar owner on Jupiter Station.

The Bar was called the Outpost, and was frequented by gas refinery employees on their mandatory off planet rotation.

"But why do people want to be somewhere else? They're already happy when they're here, they're off planet," Harksan replied.

"Because they want to be on vacation, somewhere beautiful" said Frank.

"For that they can take a cruise over the storm, it's amazing" Harksan retorted.

"Harksan, people have been looking at that storm since Galileo, I'm talking about warm weather, beautiful beaches and friendly islanders." said Frank.

"So how much does your company want?" Harksan was a bit of a no nonsense negotiator.

"My company will do it for cost, with the condition that you order a starter kit of fruit juices from our service" replied Frank.

"Oh so you take a percentage?" Harksan was getting ready to leave.

"It's not like that Harksan, it costs us about 5000 dollars to do the remodel and the first juice kit is an extra 1000, which should last 2 months. Afterwards, you can order your juice for the drinks from any provider you want, or stop selling them, though they're quite profitable. The current exchange rate of lorps to dollars is one to a hundred, so you could have the whole thing for 60 lorps, and a new look for your bar," Frank felt he was getting close.

"There are three other bars on this side of the station and one of them has a jazz band on Thursdays, though they're not very good. Why should people want to come to a Tiki Bar?" said Harksan as he cut a path straight to Frank's closer.

"Harksan I'm so glad you asked. Did I ever tell you the reason I'm in this business? When I was much younger, my wife and I honeymooned in Hawaii. It was the most beautiful and relaxing experience in my life. We went to a cultural center and we had drinks on the beach. We did the works. I do this work because I love the culture and beauty of that island so much. Every day I try to get back there. Wouldn't you like gas refiners to try and come back to your bar just as energetically?" A light rolled across Harksan's eyes and Frank's slump ended just like that. The paperwork was inconsequential and after picking a few small premiums for the remodel Frank wired the contract and credits to the corporate office. He was hoping to catch a rocket home, and called Deborah at corporate for travel arrangements.

"Hi Deborah, can I get a rocket to Cincinnati booked?"

"Hey Frank, so you finally closed one," Deborah shot back snarkily.

"I told you it was just a matter of time," said Frank, unshakeable in that moment.

"Well Mr. Welton wants to see you after you get home," she said almost with glee in her voice.

Frank nervously asked, "Do you know what it's about?"

"I think it's about something to do with new routes," she said while still somewhat too happy.

Frank knew what that meant. The trial development deal with the Soviets meant that new territory had opened up, only it was territory nobody wanted. Cold outer orbit territory. Month long rockets leaving from Jupiter with no sleeping quarters and unforgiving Russian steel seats with minimal padding. Overflowing toilets on the next RusKosmos Vostok shaking machine with meals from a tube where the best one only had a hint of cabbage. Welton might spring for second class where there were trays and silverware, but that just made the cabbage crunchier.

"Thanks Deborah, can you book a pneumatic the day after I get home?"

"Sure you don't want to drink in all that Cincinnati has to offer?" She replied even snarkier than before

"That's ok. Thanks again Deborah"

"Have a nice ride home Frank. I'm sending the boarding pass now."

He walked down to the spacedocks in the station, avoiding hobos and sitting at a wood bench right under the station clock. He looked at the boarding pass Deborah sent, third class as usual, but on Trans Galaxy third class wasn't too bad. It would be a few weeks for the flight, but the bar compartment was pretty appealing. While he didn't have a berth the Atlases usually had recliners that went all the way down. They had shower stalls and the food was pretty good.

He looked at one of the hobo's begging for change and wondered how far away he was from that life. It had gotten pretty tight after Shelly left. She had taken him to the cleaners. If not for that honeymoon trip, he'd have never thought about the line of work he was in. At some point he had almost given up and said becoming a hobo wouldn't be so bad. He had applied to DelBev as a bit of a what if and a bit of a joke. When Welton called him into his office, he had given the same spiel he gave Harksan and it had sold the deal. It was true, if not as fresh as he made it out to be, and it helped. When he'd see a new remodel, it'd take him back to his honeymoon with Shelly before it all went bad and he would smile for a second and sip a fruity drink.

The rocket announced boarding and after first class had boarded he lined up, when the astro stewardess saw his slip she motioned him aside, until all the second class passengers had gotten on. Third class was mostly beatnik kids, down on their luck spacebillies and retirees. Third class began boarding and the perfectly coiffed astro stewardess motioned him on with a thick artificial smile.

He got to his seat right next to an obese man wearing suspenders and a straw hat. Unprompted, he started telling Frank that he had come out to see his cousin at the gas refinery looking for work, but they could only let him drive a garbage shuttle, and he had better prospects earthside.

As soon as the rocket blasted off, he walked towards the bar compartment. On the wall there were posters of all the places Trans Galaxy went, the one that always caught his eye was Venus. You couldn't take an Atlas there, it had to be a saucer. They had it figured out, the whole experience was meant to be exotic. They'd always have the Botticelli Venus contorted in some way, whether coming out of the planet or holding it, but in a more cubist or modern style. Frank knew a guy in Cincinnati who had married a Venusian woman, she was always sweet and affectionate.

He pulled up a seat at the bar, which out of professional compulsion he noticed was in the modern style of the entire PanGalaxy line.

"Let me get a Manhattan, do you take dollars or lorps?"

"We take both, but to be honest we're a little tough on the exchange so you're probably better paying in dollars."

"That's fine, is there any entertainment on the flight?"

"Well first class has a new film, I think there are black and white tv's hanging down through second and third."

"What's on the tv's?"

"Oh just a rebroadcast of an Earth station, if you'd like I can get the stewardess to get you headphones."

"Yeah, is that a charge?"

"They are a little expensive but then again it's 3 weeks."

"Is there a phone?"

"This flight has one at the bar and then a small booth between here and the first class section?"

"Thanks."

"Should I charge it to your seat?"

"No, I'll pay seperately."

"That'll be 7 dollars for the headphones and a dollar for the drink?"

"Thanks."

Frank passed the days as a retiree, watching 6 hours of TV and then going to the bar. The TV had mostly reruns of the *HoneyMooners* during the day, though some of the afternoon dramas kept him occupied. He loved *Playhouse 90* at home and watching it on the small screen on the flight wasn't that different from his home life, except he had to get the drinks one at a time.

At the bar he had about 4 Manhattans per night and then snored in his seat all the way till morning. A few times he went to the phone, but he knew Shelly didn't want to hear from him. Sometimes, after a few Manhattan's, he'd get determined to call her and beg her to take him back. Then he'd remember their last fight and all his determination would fall away and he'd crawl back to his seat and start snoring.

As a rule Frank never talked to anyone in the bar compartment, not even the bartender. The three weeks finished and he ended up at Earth station. He caught a coach rocket to Cincinnati, hailed a taxi and had the robot drive him straight home.

The University Pines was a shabby apartment complex that got repainted once every three years, and was currently only at year two. Frank crawled up the stairs, set his alarm for the tube ride tomorrow, and splayed across his sometimes empty feeling queen size mattress. After the alarm rang way too early the next afternoon, he got dressed, called for a cab, and stood outside on the street. The yellow hover car arrived right at the front of the apartment and the robot driver beckoned to him.

"IDENTIFICATION"

"I'm Frank, I'm the one who called"

"ENTER AND PREPARE TO DEPART"

Frank got off at the tube station and went to the immediate boarding line. The fact that the tube was clear was soothing as it made its way across the country side. He watched as farms, suburbs, and skyscrapers whizzed by. He pulled into Grand Central and then caught a cab from the line outside to the DelBev building. It was a monolith of steel and glass with a fountain out front. He gave his name at reception and they directed him to the elevator bank on the left. Frank got out and sat in a lobby while the secretary in front of Welton's office announced him. Welton came out in a stylish black suit with a thin tie

"Frank, come on back here. Frank, have a seat, can I get you a drink?"

"I wouldn't say no to one"

"Great, we'll have a drink together." Welton poured two glasses a quarter full with scotch "Frank I just wanted to tell you we're very pleased with you here. You don't necessarily have the highest volume, but your customers keep ordering from us the longest. We value that here Frank." Frank realized the catch was coming soon. "Let me cut right to the chase, Frank. I've put a lot of thought into what we sell here at DelBev and the way I see it we sell freedom. Freedom from your daily grind, and the grayness of your daily life. That's why I'm so excited by the development deal the United States and Russia have signed. It allows each superpower to try a few ventures in the other's territory, with travel visas and permission for state companies to do contracts. Frank, the outer planets each have their own stations and those stations have quite a few bars."

"Wouldn't it be better to let some party official make that decision from Earth?"

"Well Frank, the farther out you go in the union, the more autonomy you have. By the time you get to Uranus and Neptune, you can do a lot of what you want and so each station has a lot of autonomy"

"So when do I ship out?"

"We've gotten a travel visa for you Frank. You'll get it from the embassy on Jupiter station, and then you're out to Neptune for a trial run. Oh and Frank, don't say we never got you anything, we booked you first class on the Ruskosmos." First class on a soviet rocket was almost the same as a third class ride on a Trans Galaxy or PanGalaxy flight, but then again at least it was better than nothing

"Thank you Mr. Welton"

"Thank you Frank"

The trip to Jupiter station went pretty much the same way the trip home had gone, complete with the aborted calls to Shelly, Manhattan's, and TV reruns.

When he arrived at Jupiter station, he stopped at Harksan's before going to the visa office. The name of the place had been changed to 'The Tiki Hut" and the bar had a thatched roof over it. Large tiki statues stood in the corners and one on either side of the entryway.

"Frank, doesn't it look great!" Harksan called out.

"It does Harksan, I'm glad you like it"

"What'll it be?"

"Gimme a bird of paradise."

"On the house Frank! Business is good and everybody loves the remodel. All the other bars are looking for new angles."

"That's great Harksan."

"I gotta admit Frank, I like coming into work a little more because of it, I feel like I'm travelling offworld even though it's the same old bar."

"I'm happy for you Harksan"

"It's almost like somebody gave me permission to like my job again, and so now I do."

"I'm sure it's not permission Harksan, maybe somebody just showed you how to like your job again."

"Yeah maybe that's it."

"What's Hawaii like Frank?"

"It's really nice Harksan. Though for the most part, I just stayed in the hotel, bar or took a bus trip, but it was really beautiful"

"What do you think it'd be like to live there?"

"I have no idea, but I'm sure it's nice"

"I gotta go Harksan, but thanks for the drink. " Frank left the bar, and walked toward the soviet section of the station.

"I have an appointment with the consulate"

The guard looked him over, asked for his passport, and went into the guard tower, the other guard stared at him menacingly with his hand on the rayblaster on his hip.

"Da Da, the consulate is expecting you."

He walked through the gate and down the street to the large doorway with stone and steel wrapped around it, two more guards stood at either side. In the lobby he gave his name to a receptionist. A large man walked out with a beard and wire rimmed spectacles.

"Comrade Vincenti, welcome"

"Hello, may I ask your name"

"Yaskov, I am Comrade Yaskov"

"Mr. Yaskov, it's very nice to meet you. I'm here for.."

"We know what you're here for Comrade Vincenti, may I call you Frank?"

"Sure."

"I have your transit visa right here, are you familiar with Neptune?"

"Can't really say I've ever been farther than Jupiter."

"Well Comrade, you are in luck. We will provide you with a guide for your trip."

"Oh that's not necessary!"

Yaskov got a little more serious in his tone "Oh I'm afraid I must insist. All of the economic developers are provided with one, in case your hyper translator malfunctions.

"Dimitri! Mr. Vincenti is here."

Out walked an even larger man with a thinner beard in a cheaper pea soup green suit and no spectacles.

"Hello Comrade Vincenti"

"Hello"

"I will be accompanying you on your business. I believe your rocket leaves tonight. Would you like to get some lunch?"

"So Dimitri what would you like?"

"Let's get hamburgers, Comrade Vincenti, it will be something we can remember on our Vostok ride."

"I think that's a pretty good idea, so you aren't a fan of the Ruskosmos food either."

"To not be a fan of the party's selected food on the state run rocket line would be an antisocial thing. Let's just say I have a fondness for American food when I can get it."

Dimitri smiled and Frank started trying to figure out how to use his minder to his advantage.

They sat at a booth at Big Boy Burgers, Dimitri fit tightly into the booth. After ordering, Frank began asking a few questions.

"So Dimitri, what's Neptune station like"

"I have only been there once. It was very cold and utilitarian. The State does not spend too much money on niceties."

"Do you know what I'm selling?"

"Da, Comrade Vincenti, though I am not sure you'll have a very receptive audience. Most Russians dream of visiting Havana, not Hawaii. Besides, the operator of the state's station bars is on a reasonably strict budget."

"Have you ever been to one of our remodels?"

"No, we generally don't leave the Soviet quarter of Jupiter station, and drinking on duty is considered somewhat antisocial."

"Why don't you come with me to the remodel at the station after we finish here?"

Dimitri had ordered a feast and when the bill came due he handed it to Frank. The realization that it would be his treat the rest of the way made Frank hope the dollars had been transmitted to his account from selling Harksan's remodel. They walked over to "The Tiki Hut"

"What are these things by the door?"

"That's what they call Tiki's"

"Fascinating, and the grass roof over the bar, This is really beautiful."

Harksan walked out.

"Frank, what can I get you?"

"Two birds of paradise Harksan, on me this time I insist"

"So your company makes bar's look like this?'

"Yeah it's our specialty"

"Tell me have you ever been to a place like this in real life?"

"To be honest, not really. I've been to bars made up like this. I've seen shows where they dress up the participants to look like they would belong here, but I've never seen an island with thatched huts just standing. I'm not sure it even exists any more, or if it does that it looks anything like this. My memories are of the manufactured stuff."

"That is a philosophy that we in the Soviet state wish we could employ."

Harksan brought out the drinks. Dimitri sipped his and a smile went over his face.

"What is in this?"

"Mostly pineapple juice and alcohol."

"It is delightful. Frank, you have sold me on your endeavor. Though I doubt you will be as fortunate with the operator of the state bars, it is a noble endeavor."

They walked down to the space docks and through the RusKosmos checkpoint. They sat in the lounge which looked like it had been designed in the 40's. Dimitri began smoking and offered Frank a cigarette. Frank refused for two reasons: he didn't smoke, and even if he did, Soviet cigarettes tasted terrible. First class began to board and they were shown directly to their seats. The stewardess gave a speech in Russian and then came by for a drink order, Dimitri ordered two Vodkas.

"Comrade Vincenti I'm afraid all the entertainment for this rocket will be in Russian, I could explain the movie to you…."

"That's all right Dimitri. I normally just drink and watch TV on flights."

"I can assure you that there is plenty of alcohol in First Class, but I'm afraid no one on this rocket speaks a word of English."

"Just tell them to keep me lubricated and I'll rely on your guide skills for entertainment."

The rest of first class consisted of older, obese men with bushy eyebrows and smartly dressed women who were either accompanying the men, or looked like they could kill you with their eyes. There were no shared compartments on the flight for eating or drinking, but there was a small lounge in first class for socializing.

The voyage went slowly, the Vostok shook and stewards and stewardesses routinely held on to the seat backs going up and down the rows. The films they showed were pensive with long shots of grass moving in water, or elaborate discussions. Frank decided he was going to have to break his cardinal rule and talk to Dimitri, who slept most of the day only to wake up for meals.

"So Dimitri, you said most Russians dream of Cuba, why?"

"It is the most exotic place we can dream of, visas are highly prized."

"What's the attraction to going there?"

"Much like Hawaii the appeal is warm weather, friendly islanders, and maybe some good rum."

"Do you get much of the rum?"

"In some ways we are drowning in it, it's always sent as a gift. We get a fair amount in trade, but most Russians don't even think of it when they have a drink. Nothing can compete with vodka."

"Do you really like the remodel that you saw?"

"Very much. I think since very few Russians have even seen pictures of Cuba, that they could be convinced that the islands were close to each other. In some ways seeing the bar as it was made me think that is what Havanna must look like."

"Why have you never been there?"

"I've never had the opportunity and visas are not easy to come by."

"Is it where you dream of going?"

"Not especially" Dimitri seemed uncomfortable, so Frank switched the conversation

"Do you have a family?"

"Me, No, I enjoy life too much"

"Ladies man, then?"

"You could say that Comrade Vincenti, though I think I am happiest without permanent things in my life."

"What do you do for fun then Dimitri?"

"I enjoy life, eating, drinking, and women. What more is there to do with time off?"

After saying that Dimitri hit the stewardess call button. She stumbled down the aisle and he asked her something in Russian and pinched her backside. She smiled and stumbled away.

"I've asked her for more drinks, so that we can get some sleep Comrade Vincenti"

When they arrived at Neptune station, the automated docking took over and they tapped into the station airlock. Atlases had manual docking and you could usually tell the quality of the pilot by how hard you hit the station.

They immediately washed up and Frank adjusted himself to only look mildly disheveled. The station was dark and dingy, it looked like bright colors had been banned from view.

Dimitri led the way back to a bar that was somehow darker than the rest of the station. It was completely empty. Inside he was introduced to a man with a wizard's beard. The back wall was covered with the same brand of Vodka and Frank saw instantly why this had been considered a fool's errand. He broke out his universal translator and handed the old man the other half.

"Hello, My name is Frank Vincenti, is now a good time to talk?"

"Dayes komister vincente my name is Petkov."

"Mr. Petkov, I'd like to talk to you about remodelling your bar."

"Oh the state wouldn't allow me to be so extravagant as that, I'd heard you were coming. Mr. Vincente and I am afraid you've wasted your time.

"Mr. Petkov, do you have any rum?"

"Why yes, crates of it Mr. Vincente."

"Mr. Petkov, a large number of our drinks are made with rum and fruit juices."

"You're saying your drinks get people to consume large amounts of rum."

"Yes that's correct Mr. Petkov."

"Mr. Vincente I get large amounts of rum in trade that I am never able to use, what would the remodel cost me."

"Mr. Petkov, we would consider doing the remodel for 1000 dollars if you would pre order 1 year's worth of fruit juices out to the station here for an additional 5000 dollars. I believe the state rate is 3 rubles to the dollar, so we could remodel you with a year's supply of addons for 15000 rubles."

"That is a fair amount of money, Komrister Vincente."

"Do you get many fruit juices out here Mr. Petkov?"

"No, Mr. Vincente, just rum."

"Do you think if you were decorated like this picture serving fruit juices and getting rid of free rum, your business numbers might go up?"

"Yes Mr. Vincente I do, can I make a proposal?"

"Of course Mr. Petkov."

"If you give me the remodel for the cost of just supplies, and business is successful, I'll do the same deal for two other bars on this station and one on Uranus."

"Mr. Petkov, I'll take that deal instantly."

Frank's commission was always on the juices and he had just made his yearly quota. Dimitri wired the embassy the contract and they wired it through to Frank's office. Welton sent a good job in the reply and Frank began making plans for home.There was a saucer heading direct from the station for venus and he felt he'd earned it.

Made in the USA
Las Vegas, NV
17 May 2025